Hi, I'm Poppy!
Reading new books is fun ... will
always love my old favou... stories,
but I love to read about ...
characters, different w... and
exciting adventures. Be... ding
princess just like me!

Love Poppy × × ×

P.S. Why not try ...king your
own bookmark?

Make Your Own
Bookmark

1. Cut some thick card into a
strip of about 4 cm by 12 cm

2. Cut the bottom into a
triangular shape

3. Decorate using paints with
coloured pencils or fine-line
pens

4. You can draw a scene from
your favourite story or your
favourite character

5. Why not write a few words
from your very favourite story

6. These make lovely gifts for
friends!

Honeysuckle Cottage
Poppy's House

Forget-Me-Not Cottage
Grandpa's House and Office

Poppy Field

N
W E
S

Honeypot Cottage
Honey and Granny Bumble's House

Blossom
Bakehouse

Cornsilk Castle
and Courtyard

Re-Bloom
Boutique

Village Hall

Sage's
Vet Surgery

Post Office

River Swan

Beehive
Beauty Salon

Barley Farm
The Meadowsweets' House

Riverside
Stables

Honeypot Hill
Railway Station

To Camomile Cove
via Periwinkle Lane

*Visit Princess Poppy for fun, games, puzzles,
activities, downloads and lots more at:*

www.princesspoppy.com

STORYTELLING PRINCESS
A PICTURE CORGI BOOK 978 0 552 57136 4
Published in Great Britain by Picture Corgi,
an imprint of Random House Children's Publishers UK
A Penguin Random House Company

Penguin
Random House
UK

This edition published 2015
1 3 5 7 9 10 8 6 4 2
Text copyright © Janey Louise Jones, 2015
Illustrations copyright © Picture Corgi Books, 2015
Illustrations by Veronica Vasylenko
PRINCESS POPPY is a registered trade mark of The Random House Group Limited.
The right of Janey Louise Jones and Veronica Vasylenko to be identified as the author and illustrator
of this work has been asserted in accordance with the Copyright, Designs and Patents Act 1988.
All rights reserved.
Picture Corgi Books are published by Random House Children's Publishers UK,
61–63 Uxbridge Road, London W5 5SA

www.princesspoppy.com
www.randomhousechildrens.co.uk

Addresses for companies within The Random House Group Limited can be found at: www.randomhouse.co.uk/offices.htm
THE RANDOM HOUSE GROUP Limited Reg. No. 954009
A CIP catalogue record for this book is available from the British Library.
Printed in China

Penguin Random House is committed to a sustainable future for our business, our readers and our planet.
This book is made from Forest Stewardship Council® certified paper.

MIX
Paper from
responsible sources
FSC® C020056
FSC
www.fsc.org

Storytelling Princess

Written by Janey Louise Jones

PICTURE CORGI

For a great teacher, Judy Hayman,
who inspired me with words and stories.

★

Storytelling Princess

featuring

Honey

★

Princess Poppy

★

Sweetpea

★

Miss Mallow

★

Mum

★

Mimosa

★

Jonny

★

Poppy and her friends were getting very excited —
next week was Reading Week at Rosehip School, and
on Friday there was to be a special dress-up party.

"I love all these dresses and costumes!" said Poppy.
"How will I ever choose one for Reading Week?"

"Let's all dress as our very favourite character and
say why we like her!" said Sweetpea.

Luckily everyone had a different favourite.

"I love Alice," said Poppy, "because she has a really BIG imagination!"

"Little Red Riding Hood is my favourite," said Honey. "She loves her granny just like I do!"

"I like the Little Mermaid because I love swimming," said Mimosa.

"I'm going to be the Fairy Godmother because I want to grant wishes," said Sweetpea.

"Reading Week will be fun!" said Honey. "I've finished the story Miss Mallow gave me to read already!"

"Same here!" said Sweetpea. "I read it all by myself. Have you read your story yet, Poppy?"

"Um . . . a bit," Poppy mumbled, then changed the subject. "I know — I'll make up a story for us right now!"

"Cool!" chorused the other girls.

All the friends sat in a circle
and Poppy began to tell a story . . .
    "One day in Honeypot
Hill, right by Bumble Bee's
Teashop, a fairy bumped
into a princess . . ."

"And then what happened?"
asked Honey.
    "They rode on winged
ponies to a magical castle!"
continued Poppy.

"What did they
do there?" asked
Sweetpea.

"They met their friends – other princesses and fairies – and they made petal perfume and then danced until dawn," said Poppy. "And the grown-ups didn't even realise there was a party!"

The girls giggled, imagining a secret party of their own.

On Sunday, Poppy tried to read *The Silver Pony*, the book Miss Mallow had given her to talk about in class on Wednesday. But Poppy didn't really feel like reading.

"Shall we read it together?" suggested Mum.

Poppy hesitated. "No, I can manage by myself, thanks," she said. "Reading aloud is for babies."

"You're never too old for story time," said Mum. "But it's up to you."

Poppy tried to read her book again at bedtime, but she decided
to read her favourite book of fairytales instead.

Her head was filled with princesses, castles, enchanted forests
and talking animals. Soon she fell into a dreamy sleep . . .

Poppy had such a busy time at school during Reading Week.
There were all sorts of fun activities.

Monday morning: Meet the author.

Monday afternoon: Sing-along story time.

Tuesday morning: Help the school librarian to place newly arrived books.

Tuesday afternoon: Make a poster about your favourite book character.

Time flew by and soon it was Wednesday.

"We're halfway through our celebration of reading," said Miss Mallow. "That means we'll hear everybody's book reviews after break!"

Oh no! thought Poppy. *I still haven't read my book!*

Poppy spent all of break trying to read *The Silver Pony,* but she was too worried and couldn't concentrate. It was too late!

"Who wants to go first?" asked Miss Mallow. Poppy blushed bright red. What was she going to do?

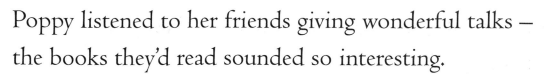

Poppy listened to her friends giving wonderful talks –
the books they'd read sounded so interesting.
Sweetpea spoke about a kindly wizard
whose spells never worked.

Honey spoke about
a ballerina who lost
her confidence then
found it again.

And Jonny spoke about
a football hero.

Poppy felt sick with nerves. *Why, oh why, did I not read it as I was told?* she said to herself crossly.

"Who's next . . . Poppy?" asked Miss Mallow.

Poppy stood in front of the class with burning bright cheeks.

"My book is called *The Silver Pony*. There's a little pony whose coat is the shiniest silver ..." Poppy began. But she didn't really know anything else so she decided to make it up.

"She is magical... she can fly... "

"Poppy!" said Miss Mallow. "That doesn't sound like *The Silver Pony* to me! Are you sure you've read it?"

Poppy shook her head.

"I did try to read it," said Poppy quickly, "but I've been reading fairytales and making up stories instead. And thinking about what I'll wear on Friday. I'm very sorry!"

Miss Mallow looked disappointed, but not angry.

"Okay, everybody," she said. "It's time for some personal reading."

Then she took Poppy aside.

"Poppy, you tell the most wonderful stories, but now I'd like you to read one with me. I think you will love it if you give it a try!"

Poppy settled on a beanbag and Miss Mallow sat beside her.

"How about we take turns to read aloud?" suggested Miss Mallow.

Poppy nodded and they began.

As Poppy and Miss Mallow read
The Silver Pony together,
the book seemed to
spring to life.

"Isn't she an amazing
little pony?" said
Miss Mallow.

But Poppy's eyes were glued to the page. She couldn't wait to see what happened next.

Soon it was Friday, and time for the dress-up party in the school hall. But all Poppy wanted to do was sit and read her new favourite book, *The Silver Pony*.

And by the end of school Poppy had told her friends the whole story of the little pony – and she didn't have to make up one thing!

By bedtime that night, Poppy had finished reading *The Silver Pony* for the third time. Mum even let her read it to Angel and Archie as their bedtime story.

Once the twins were asleep, Mum snuggled up with Poppy for her bedtime story.

"Can I make up my own story for you now, Mum?" asked Poppy.

Mum kissed Poppy on the forehead. "Of course you can,
my storytelling princess!" she whispered, and Poppy began her tale.

Once upon a time
long ago